BUGGED OUT!

CHOOSE YOUR OWN

NIGHTMARE... #8

BUGGED OUT!
BY LABAN CARRICK HILL

ILLUSTRATED BY BILL SCHMIDT

An R. A. Montgomery Book

BANTAM BOOKS
NEW YORK · TORONTO · LONDON · SYDNEY · AUCKLAND

RL 4, age 008–012

BUGGED OUT!

A Bantam Book/April 1996

CHOOSE YOUR OWN NIGHTMARE™ is a trademark of
Bantam Doubleday Dell Books for Young Readers,
a division of Bantam Doubleday Dell Publishing Group, Inc.
Registered in U.S. Patent and Trademark Office and elsewhere.

Cover and interior illustrations by Bill Schmidt
Cover and interior design by Beverly Leung

ISBN 0-553-48326-9

Published simultaneously in the United States and Canada

Bantam Books are published by Bantam Books, a division of
Bantam Doubleday Dell Publishing Group, Inc. Its trademark,
consisting of the words "Bantam Books" and the portrayal of a
rooster, is Registered in U.S. Patent and Trademark Office and in
other countries. Marca Registrada. Bantam Books, 1540 Broadway,
New York, New York 10036.

PRINTED IN THE UNITED STATES OF AMERICA

OPM   0   9   8   7   6   5   4   3   2   1

BUGGED OUT!

WARNING!

You have probably read books where scary things happen to people. Well, in *Choose Your Own Nightmare*, you're right in the middle of the action. The scary things are happening to you!

Did you hear the latest buzz at school? You're a fly! But don't let it bug you.

Fortunately, while you're reading along, you'll have chances to decide what to do. Whenever you make a decision, turn to the page shown. The thrills and chills that happen to you next will depend on your choices.

It's important to choose carefully. You wouldn't want to get swatted.

"Have you ever put your face real close to a gray, slippery, slimy slug? Real, real close?" Emily, your best friend, asks you.

That's what she wants you to do right now. She has spied two oozing, snotlike slugs munching heartily on a rotten tomato in your backyard. She bends over and waves for you to do the same.

"Yuck!" you scream. "I hate those things."

"Oh, come on, they're just slugs." Emily sticks her finger into a gob of the slug slime. She brings her finger up to her nose and smells it.

"I think I'm going to throw up," you say.

"What's wrong? Are you sick?" she asks.

You just shake your head in disgust. "I can do without bugs. They're gross."

"How can you say that?" Emily cries.

"Here we go again," you mutter under your breath. Emily is crazy about bugs. You can't stand them. It's the only thing the two of you don't agree on.

Turn to page 2.

She continues. "If you pour salt on a slug, it melts. But that's really cruel because they don't do anything to you. Did you know that two-thirds of the animals on earth are bugs?" Emily picks up one of the slugs and watches it slither across her fingers.

"Ugh! Now I *know* I'm going to throw up," you repeat as you nearly lose it. "Give me the third that aren't bugs and I'll be happy."

Luckily, just then your mother opens the screen door and calls you in. "Suuuupp-ppperrrr!"

"See ya, Emily. Sorry I couldn't stay out longer," you add. But you're secretly relieved that it's dinnertime. From past experience, you know that Emily was about to go off on her favorite subject—BUGS!

"Good luck in the play tomorrow," she yells as she runs across the yard.

You head for your back door. The last thing you want to think about is that play—you're stuck playing a dinosaur. Your teacher, Mrs. Whittemore, tricked you into the part, and you have a major case of stage fright.

Go on to the next page.

Inside the house, your bratty little brother, Jake, is pouring your milk into his glass. You tweak his nose and slide into the chair beside him. On the table is a platter heaped with liver, onions, and brussels sprouts.

Your dad lays a good-sized slab of liver on your plate. It looks exactly like a slippery, giant brown slug.

"I'm really getting sick now," you mumble.

"What's that, honey?" your mom asks.

You simply shake your head.

"Don't forget to tell him about the package from Uncle Bill," your dad interrupts.

"What package?" you ask excitedly.

"Eat your supper," your mom answers. "There's plenty of time for Uncle Bill's shenanigans afterward." She gives your dad a withering look.

From past experience you know that if you bring up your uncle's package again you might never get it. You focus on trying to swallow pieces of liver without actually tasting it. You cut the meat into tiny pieces, open your mouth wide, and place a small sliver on the back of your tongue.

Turn to page 4.

4

"Ughhh!" You gag and start to cough. Worried that you might be choking, your dad reaches over and slaps your back hard.

"Don't," you wheeze as you spit the liver onto your mother's lap.

Gasping, you try to apologize, but your mom simply shakes her head.

"If you would just eat your food like a normal person, you wouldn't choke! Now I want you to clean this mess up and finish your sprouts before you go upstairs and open Uncle Bill's package."

Jake giggles and runs from the dining room, while you clear the table. Tonight was supposed to be Jake's night to clean up.

When everything is finished, you yell to your parents in the living room, "I'm done. Can I go upstairs now?"

"Okay, but make sure you practice your lines for tomorrow's play!" your dad calls back.

Go on to the next page.

A shiver runs down your spine, and you try to push the thought of the play out of your mind. But you can't. Just the idea of going on that stage dressed up as a dinosaur makes you want to disappear or run away—anything but show up at school tomorrow.

You try to put it out of your mind as you climb the stairs to your bedroom.

On your desk is a large, battered box. It's sitting on top of a mess of schoolbooks, a catcher's mitt, and some video games. The box looks as if it has traveled around the world to get here, and it nearly has. Uncle Bill is an anthropologist. Right now he's studying a lost tribe deep in Brazil's Amazon rain forest.

You take out a penknife, cut the strange, beautiful stamps off the upper right corner of the package, and tack them onto your bulletin board. You collect stamps—you've got dozens from all over the world. Then you slip the blade under the tape and cut the box flaps free.

Turn to page 32.

6

"H-How c-can this be?" she stutters in shock. "This fly has blond hair!" You know Emily is aware that all flies are covered with tiny black hairs. Hairs just like those on the mask.

She peers more closely at you as you perch below the magnifying glass. She keeps repeating under her breath, "Blond hair, blond hair, blond hair."

You want to scream, "Enough already!" but you know that she's just beginning to recognize you. So you sit as still as a fly can sit, which unfortunately isn't too still. You twitch and rub your legs together and stick your tongue out and make small hops as if you've got a nervous tic. But you're just a fly, and that's what flies do.

Emily continues to talk to herself. "There's a nose . . . and there's human eyes . . . and human ears . . . and . . . and . . . blond hair."

You scream, "Would you wake up, Emily! It's me! It's me! Yes, I'm not a fly. I'm really a human." But all that comes out is that irritating buzz flies make. Your voice has changed completely into a fly's.

"Is that *you*?" she asks hesitantly.

Turn to page 17.

A sudden scream pulls you out of your reverie. "Bugs!"

You've been spotted. The air whistles beside you, sending you reeling toward the floor.

Your face smashes against the leg of a chair. You're dizzy and off balance, but your head clears quickly and you realize you'd better move. Move. Move! You fly low, close to the floor, toward the door.

But the door is closed. You're caught.

You spot a crack at the bottom of the door. Dive. Dive. Dive!

"Whew!" you gasp. "Made it."

The nurses in the nursery are glaring at you through the window, ready if you decide to return.

You beat it down the hall as fast as you can.

Suddenly a delicious smell hits you. You can't quite figure out what the aroma is, but it draws you into a large room.

"Food!" you scream.

You've found the hospital cafeteria. A long counter holds tray upon tray of warm food— fried mystery meat, Day-Glo orange macaroni and cheese, reconstituted mashed potatoes.

Turn to page 65.

8

You're bored from waiting so long. And you're sure that Emily has already left the hospital. You realize your best bet is to return home and hopefully meet up with her there.

But first you've got to get something to eat. You're starving. You wonder what flies eat. It's something you really don't want to find out. You figure you can just as easily sneak into a restaurant and get a few bites of regular food without anyone noticing. The only problem is that there are no restaurants around, just warehouses.

You decide to scout around. There must be a deli somewhere nearby. As you fly down the block, you pass building after building with brick facades and small gray steel doors. None of them resembles a restaurant or deli.

It doesn't take long before you're ready to give up and head for home. Then a distinctly appealing smell attracts your attention. It's a sweetish-sour aroma that tickles your nose and gets your stomach growling.

Turn to page 15.

In a panic you fly downstairs to the kitchen.

Your mom is at the counter fixing your school lunch. The makings of your favorite sandwich are spread out on the counter: bacon, bologna, lettuce, and tomato. Four pieces of bread are laid out in a row. Your mom is spreading each with mayonnaise.

Hungry, you feel a nearly uncontrollable urge to dive straight into a slice of juicy, ripe, red tomato. The succulent flesh of the tomato calls out to you. Its heady aroma is almost too powerful to resist.

Luckily you come to your senses before you dive-bomb the tomatoes. Instead you buzz up to your mom's face to get her attention, but your mom automatically swats you away. She's not even aware you're there.

You circle her head and try to yell in her ear. "Bzzz!" you buzz frantically. But she brushes you off again.

In desperation, you land on her nose.

"Ahhh!" she screams. She jumps in surprise and swats you off as hard as she can.

Turn to page 12.

"Hmmm. A rare example of the *Diptera transmograe*," the old man says in an odd Viennese accent. He shines a bright light in your face and observes you closely.

"The eyes dilate like a human's," he says out loud to nobody in particular.

He takes a pair of tweezers and gently turns you on your back. He pokes you with the tweezers and then looks up at the group.

"No doubt about it," he says. "This fly is a human being."

"Brilliant," you say sarcastically, knowing that no one understands what you're saying. You're getting restless and hungry while this doctor is discovering the obvious. You feel the urge to go for a short spin around the room, and so you lift off.

"Sit," the doctor suddenly commands. You didn't even think he was looking at you. Nevertheless, you obey.

"Can your friend understand me?" the man asks Emily.

Emily answers, "Yes, sir."

The man pulls up a stool, sits in front of you, and adjusts a huge magnifying glass.

Turn to page 37.

You start to write: *S, C* . . . Emily nods and heads for the door.

"I need to go home first. I forgot my math book," she says. You follow her out the back door of the house.

"Are you and Emily leaving for school?" your mom calls out after you.

Emily stops dead in her tracks. You look at each other, wondering what to say. "Yes! But we can't stop, or we'll be late for school!" Emily hollers.

You hear your mom reply but you can't make out what's she's saying because you and Emily are already through the door. When you reach Emily's house, you hurry upstairs.

As you pass her mom's bedroom, a voice calls out, "Emily, don't be late for school."

"I won't, Mom," Emily answers as she dashes into her bedroom. Quickly she stops to make her bed and brush her hair.

"And don't come up the stairs like a herd of elephants. How many times do I have to tell you?"

"All *right,* Mom," Emily says automatically, without having heard what her mom said.

Turn to page 84.

12

You fall off balance, flapping your wings and trying to recover. But you can't. Instead, you drop directly into a blob of mayonnaise that's about to be spread on a piece of bread.

"Get off there!" your mom screams, raising her hand as if to crush you.

You try to fly away, but the mayo is too heavy and sticky and you can't lift off. Quickly you roll off the edge of the bread. You try to catch your breath as your mother smashes a second piece of bread on top of the piece you'd landed on. That was close, you think worriedly.

Finally you get airborne again, just as your mom smashes her hand onto the spot on the counter where you were perched.

"Gotcha!" she yells with satisfaction.

Then she lifts her hand and sees the clean countertop. No bug guts. "Missed!" she mutters, disappointed. "Next time I'll be prepared."

Your mom opens the broom closet and pulls out a flyswatter. She means business.

Turn to page 31.

14

"It's all your fault I'm late, you little insect," Emily says as quietly as she can. "My mom's going to kill me."

"Now, class, as you know, after school today we have a class play. I expect everyone to be here on . . ." Mrs. Whittemore stops midsentence and looks around the room. "We're missing our dinosaur!"

Emily buries her head on her desk.

"Emily," Mrs. Whittemore calls. "Where is our dinosaur?"

"Sick," Emily answers without lifting her face. She's afraid Mrs. Whittemore will see she's lying.

"This is a major catastrophe!" Mrs. Whittemore moans. "We don't have an understudy and the dinosaur is the biggest part."

Afraid that Mrs. Whittemore might call your home, Emily adds, "I think the dinosaur will feel better this afternoon. Don't worry. I'm sure we'll both be at the play."

Angrily, you fly to Emily's ear and buzz as loudly as you can. The best thing about being a fly is that you'll *miss* the play. You hate it when Emily makes promises you don't want to keep.

Turn to page 52.

Without a moment's thought, you're off. "Suppertime!" you yell to no one in particular. You fly with the fury of someone who hasn't eaten in days. Your entire minuscule body is screaming for food. You can't understand what's going on. All you know is that you've got to get to that food now.

The smell gets stronger and stronger as you fly toward it. You're drawn to it as if it were a powerful magnet. You have no control over your body as it wings its way toward that delicious fragrance.

All along the way you keep asking yourself: What is it? What is that marvelous perfume? You round the corner. Your eyes lock on the feast. It's a dream. It's perfection. It's . . .

A dark green Dumpster full of rotting food!

A Dumpster is the last thing you could ever imagine liking. But there is no getting around it. You desperately want to dive into that stinky, slimy, disgusting garbage.

If you decide you must bathe in the rotting garbage, turn to page 44.

If you feel you can resist the putrid Dumpster, turn to page 46.

16

In the lab Mr. Scully is hurrying around the room, collecting test tubes from the last class and handing out clean ones for the next. As usual the tail of his shirt is sticking out the back of his pants, his sleeves are rolled unevenly up his arms, and it looks as if he shaved only half his face this morning.

Emily pushes past the kids coming in. "Mr. Scully! Mr. Scully!" she yells.

Mr. Scully looks up and sees her. "You know you promised not to skip classes to spend more time in the lab," he says, shaking his head in disappointment. "You don't belong in here until after lunch. Now go!" He turns away to finish setting up for the next class.

"But wait!" Emily pleads. "This is an emergency!"

"We'll talk about it during class time after lunch," Mr. Scully responds.

If you decide to buzz loudly to get Mr. Scully's attention, turn to page 58.

If you're certain Mr. Scully won't change his mind, turn to page 75.

All you can do to answer is buzz. You fly over to the window again, hoping she'll follow. You drag your body across the wet, frosted window and spell out *HELP!* Then you fall to the windowsill, too heavy with water to fly.

Now Emily gets it. She runs over to the window and traces the letters you've just written with her fingers. Her hand unconsciously slaps the windowsill.

Smack.

You wince. If this keeps up, you're going to have the most awful headache. That was a close call. Emily's hand lands within millimeters of where you are lying, helplessly sodden with dew.

"Oh, no!" she screams, quickly lifting her hand.

You brace for another hit, but Emily simply brings her hand up to her mouth. She's just realized how close she came to making bug juice out of you.

Turn to page 60.

18

"Well, I'm not sure what we can do," Mr. Scully answers thoughtfully. "How do you two communicate?"

"He understands everything you say and can write by dipping his leg into ink," Emily explains.

Mr. Scully pours a few drops of ink from his fountain pen onto a piece of paper. "Now first you need to promise to do all your homework and show up for my classes on time," he tells you.

You sit there, not quite understanding what he's talking about.

Mr. Scully turns to Emily and says irritably, "I thought he could write."

"He can," Emily answers.

"Well, tell your friend to promise to be a perfect student in my classes and no more fooling around. Otherwise . . ."

Before Mr. Scully can finish his sentence, you're writing, *PROMISE!*

Turn to page 25.

Emily tries to add a little humor to the situation. "I know you didn't want to be in the play, but this is sure a strange way to get out of it!"

You dip a leg in the ink. *NOT FUNNY,* you write.

Emily laughs at her own joke. "We'd better do something quick," she says. "We need help."

DON'T TELL MOM, you implore. The last thing you want is to be a grounded fly. You collapse. Writer's cramp has made your whole body stiff.

"I won't," she assures you. She bends down close. "Listen," she says, "there's a couple of things we can do. But it's really your choice. We can go to the hospital and see if they can help. Or we can go see Mr. Scully at school. He's a crack entomologist. He taught me everything I know about bugs."

You hate the idea of making a decision. Do you see a doctor or an insect expert? Are you still a human? Or are you a bug?

If you decide you're more human than bug, turn to page 21.

If you conclude that you're more bug than human, turn to page 11.

You carefully lift the mask out of the box. In your hurry to put it on, you don't notice the fine dust—like grains of wheat—that settles on your face, hair, and shoulders.

The mask fastens behind your head with little leather straps. When you get it in place, you peer into the mirror over the dresser. You look like a giant fly from some horror movie! Silvery, gogglelike eyes dominate the black, triangular face. You laugh. Even though you hate bugs—*especially* flies—you have to admit the mask is pretty cool.

Still wearing the mask, you call Emily on the phone to tell her about your present from Uncle Bill.

"You've got to come over right away to see it."

"It sounds great!" she says. "But I can't. I've got to do my math homework. Besides," she adds sarcastically, "you need all the rest you can get to be ready for the play tomorrow."

"You're going to pay," you warn.

"Morning, dude," Emily answers and hangs up.

Turn to page 70.

You dip your leg one more time into the ink and begin to write: *H, O* . . .

Before you get any further, Emily runs out of the room, calling you to follow her. She dashes out of the house as you pursue her, flying as fast as you can. Thank goodness your mom is doing laundry in the basement.

Emily marches down the street toward the bus stop at the corner, with you buzzing close behind. "A doctor should be able to figure this out," she tells you. "Don't worry."

As you wait for the bus, a strange—but incredibly wonderful—smell wafts past your nostrils. Your whole body begins to twitch in excitement. You are looking around trying to find the source of this marvelous smell when you see Emily's golden retriever trotting down the street toward you. You don't understand—Emily's dog stinks. Or at least that's what you've always thought . . . until now!

As the dog nears the bus stop, you have an uncontrollable urge to fly over to it. So you do. You circle the dog's head. You land on his back, drinking in the glorious aroma. It's better than any expensive perfume.

Turn to page 36.

At the hospital you and Emily barge through the emergency room door.

Emily walks up to the nurses' station. "I have an emergency," she says.

A large, hulking nurse who looks like a linebacker for the Green Bay Packers glances at Emily. "You don't look sick. What's wrong?"

"It's not me. It's my friend." Emily points to you hovering beside her.

"We don't have time for jokes," the nurse says as she walks away.

"No, I'm serious!" Emily yells, but the nurse ignores her. Emily lays her head on the counter, totally discouraged.

You land on Emily's hand and buzz really loudly. You've got an idea.

Emily figures out that you want to talk and steals a pen from the counter. You both head over to the waiting room, which is packed with people. Emily grabs a magazine to write on and breaks open the pen.

You dip your leg in the ink and write, TELL THEM YOU'RE SICK.

"But the doctor will know nothing's wrong with me," Emily answers.

Turn to page 69.

Frantically you lean forward, in hopes of somehow stabilizing, when something abruptly stops you in midair.

"What's going on?" you scream.

You've been grabbed! You are being held tightly a foot off the ground about four inches from the brick wall. You twist to break free, but the grip on you only strengthens. You try to turn to find out what's holding you but see nothing. It's as if something invisible has snatched you out of the air.

You panic, and your heart begins to race. Your legs twitch uncontrollably. You can't seem to get a grip on yourself at all.

Then you see it. A faint glimmer reflects the fine threads of a spider's web. It's your worst nightmare. You know you have no chance of breaking free, but you twist and pull anyway. You have no choice. You must escape from this sticky web.

As you writhe on the web, you realize that the more you struggle, the more entangled you become. Finally you slump, out of breath. I have to think, you tell yourself. I have to calm down. Otherwise I might never break free.

Turn to page 47.

"Better watch where I land or I'm history!" you buzz out loud. "Whoa!" you yell as you leap again and fall three feet to the floor, landing on your back. Emily has come over to the sink and startled you.

"Are you okay?" she asks.

You struggle to flip over. Then you fly up to her hand. "Yeah," you buzz, trying to nod.

"Wait," says Emily. "I can't understand you. Let's find something to write with." She goes to the wall of cabinets and tries to open them. They're all locked.

"I guess we're just going to have to wait for the doctor," she says, disappointed.

A few minutes go by. "Where is this doctor?" Emily asks impatiently.

You feel the same way. You can't stand to wait any longer. Your mom always tells you you have no patience, but this is an emergency. You're not sure what to do. Should you wait with Emily, where it's safe? Or should you find out what's taking so long?

*To find out what the delay is,
turn to page 26.*

*To wait it out with Emily,
turn to page 80.*

Mr. Scully nods in satisfaction and turns to the class that has just entered the room. "Class, we're going to have a pop quiz. Everybody put your books away and answer the following questions." Mr. Scully writes several questions on the board about the digestive tracts of worms and frogs. You can hear a number of grunts and groans from students in the classroom.

"He's got the class busy for a while so he can work on you," Emily whispers.

Mr. Scully taps a petri dish, indicating that you should sit in it. When you land, he pours a sticky, sweet-tasting liquid in it that nearly drowns you. It coats your wings so that you can't fly, but you don't mind because it tastes so good.

Next, Mr. Scully lifts you up with a pair of tweezers. It feels as if he's going to crush you, but instead he drops you on a glass slide and places you under his microscope.

"Never in my life . . . ," Mr. Scully mumbles. "How in the world . . ."

Turn to page 34.

26

You notice that the door to the room is cracked open, so you decide to scout around to see what you can find. You slip through the door and accidentally fly into a huge head of hair. It's like a jungle. There's so much hair you get tangled up in it and can't free yourself.

As you twist and turn, trying to break loose, the head moves quickly down the hall and through a pair of swinging doors. The hair is sticky with hairspray and smells sickeningly sweet. With your every move each individual hair seems to wrap around you and pull your body farther in.

While you struggle, the head of hair continues to move along quickly, until suddenly everything goes dark. What's going on? You calm down when you realize the person has put on some kind of hat. It has elastic around the edges. No light seeps through the sides.

You hear muffled voices. You can barely make out what they are saying.

"Okay, everybody," says someone. "Let's cut him open. We've got to get that kidney out right away."

Turn to page 53.

Without thinking, you leap into the air and swoop up high toward the ceiling. You quickly give up on the idea of ever convincing your mom that you're you in a fly's body.

For safety you hide in the light fixture attached to the ceiling. You're certain your mom can't reach up there without standing on a chair. The warmth of the lightbulb is comforting—so much so that you land on it.

"Yeeooowwweeee!" you scream in a voice no one but a fly can understand. You've burned your little fly feet on the hot bulb! So *that's* why there are always dead flies and moths in the ceiling fixtures. They get fried by the hot lightbulbs. You never realized how dangerous the life of a fly could be until now.

Your singed feet are throbbing with pain. It feels as if they're still cooking. You've got to cool them off. But where?

Fortunately, you remember the tomatoes. The cool, wet tomatoes. They're perfect for soothing six fried feet.

Turn to page 85.

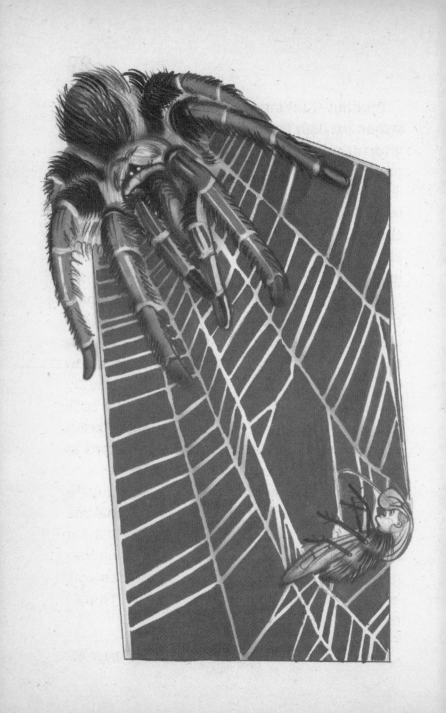

By the way it's looking at you, you can tell it's angry. You've enraged it by not letting it wrap you in a cocoon. But more importantly, you can tell it's hungry. The spider is staring at you as if you're a three-course meal!

With its eyes locked on you, the spider slowly crawls down the web, taking its own sweet time. Violently thrashing against your constraints, you feel a leg suddenly break free. You go nuts. You jerk your body as hard as you can. Two more legs come loose.

A ray of hope rises in you. You glance up at the spider and see it methodically approaching. It's taking its time.

You writhe in response and pull your back partially off the web. Your excitement rises. You work even harder. More of you begins to break free!

You lose sight of the spider as you struggle. You don't know how close it is to you. All you know is that it's a race you must win.

Suddenly, out of nowhere, the spider pounces. Its eight powerful legs embrace you. You feel a slight prick, almost a bite. Numbness flows through your body. . . .

The End

Unexpectedly, you're distracted by a strange odor. It's a bitter smell, very different from the cheese and noodles. You don't recognize it, but you can feel your whole body being drawn toward it. You twist and slide down a macaroni tube, and there it is . . .

Delicate hairlike growths, invisible to the human eye but not to your fly eyes. You squirm over to it, curious about what it might be. You've never seen anything like it. Each hair seems to be spurting thousands and thousands of little organisms that look just like the photographs in your science book at school.

And it smells so good!

You give it a lick. Then another. The taste is somehow familiar, and you wonder where you've tasted it before. Then it comes to you. This is mold. This tastes like moldy cheese.

"*Yuck!*" you howl. But it *is* good.

Before you realize what is happening, your body begins to grumble as if it has a giant stomachache. It feels as if the mold is reproducing inside you. You're going to explode!

Your skin gets tighter and tighter as your stomach expands. The pain is unbearable.

Turn to page 72.

You hover above the kitchen cabinets, aghast at your mom's mean streak. You've discovered for the first time who your mom really is: a bloodthirsty insect murderer!

How are you going to get through to her? She's your mom. And she always has the right answer to every problem, no matter how strange. You know she can help . . .

Swooossshhhh!

The flyswatter just missed you. You've got to think fast. Can you get your mom's attention long enough to communicate that you're her kid? Or would it be better to retreat to the safety of your room until you can figure out the best course of action?

If you think you can convince your mom that you've turned into a fly, turn to page 54.

If you decide to retreat and fly out of the kitchen, turn to page 56.

"Wow!" you whisper in awe. Nested among dried grass is the most incredible mask you've ever seen. You quickly pull out your uncle's letter.

Greetings!

Thought you would like this! It's a mask used in the worship of a tiny fly from the <u>Diptera transmograe</u> family. The ceremonies are secret, and I haven't been able to find out much about them. Legend has it that people turn into flies. The mask itself is covered with hair from thousands of flies, glued on with sticky fly spit. It can take as much as a year to make one of these masks. I'll keep you posted when I find out more about how the mask is used.

Miss you,
Uncle Bill

Turn to page 20.

He flattens out your wings with the tweezers and then nearly pokes your eye out.

"Ouch!" you shout when he pulls out a hair.

"What was that?" Mr. Scully looks up. "Did your friend say something?" he whispers to Emily.

"Well, it's hard to tell, but usually when he's buzzing he's talking, I think," she says, shrugging.

Mr. Scully scratches his head. "So . . . still has the power of speech . . . even if he can't articulate in an understandable way." He drops you back in the petri dish headfirst. You swallow a mouthful of the sweet liquid and gag. You wonder if they can do the Heimlich maneuver on a fly. If so, now is the time.

"The cell structure is odd for a fly," Mr. Scully explains to Emily. "In fact, the cell walls are polysaccharide, which is highly unusual. This would suggest that these cells are malleable, or rather, changeable."

"What are you talking about?" Emily asks.

Turn to page 61.

"Has someone called this fly's mother?" one doctor asks, ignoring Emily's question.

Everybody looks at each other, hoping someone else has called.

Dr. Joyce turns to Emily. "We need your friend's home phone number."

Emily tries to object, but another doctor cuts her off, explaining that they can't help you unless they get a parent's permission. She relents and gives them your number.

It isn't long before your mom comes crashing into the room with your younger brother, Jake, in tow. But they're not alone. Behind them an old man creeps in. He looks like an undertaker in his crisp white shirt and dark suit, but it's clear that the other doctors respect him. They step aside as he approaches.

Your mom pushes Jake out of the room and tells him to wait outside.

As Jake scoots out, you notice he's holding the fly mask. You want to tell someone to get it away from him before he turns into a fly, too. But you know no one will understand you. You pray that your little brother isn't dumb enough to put the mask on.

Turn to page 10.

"Oh no!" you gasp. You really are a fly. This is exactly the kind of smell a fly would like!

Emily calls, "Come on! The bus is here."

As she steps onto the bus, she waves for you to follow.

The bus driver looks past her and sees the dog. "No dogs on the bus!"

Emily stares at him as if he's crazy and pays her fare. You dart through an open window and follow her to a seat in the back.

You can tell this is going to be a long bus ride, and you're not sure whether you're up for it. You're having second thoughts. This hospital idea doesn't sound too promising. What help can a doctor give you? You're confused about what to do. The more you think about it, the more discouraged you feel.

If you go with Emily to the hospital, turn to page 22.

If you decide to go along with Emily only until you can come up with a better idea, turn to page 42.

"My name is Dr. Mowbray, and I'm a specialist in entomology. In other words, bugs."

You nod, and you get the distinct feeling that he sees you do it.

"My specialty has been isolating the sight gene in flies." He coughs. "You might have heard of my latest experiment, in which I grew eyes on the wings and legs of flies?"

You nod even though you haven't heard of his work.

"Well," Dr. Mowbray continues with a little chuckle, "your problem is a little more difficult than simply altering genes."

He slips a piece of stationery out of his pocket. He adjusts his glasses and turns to your mother. "Madam, I regret to say that I can't help your son unless you sign this release form."

Your mother stands as still as a statue, listening.

Dr. Mowbray continues. "You see, I can't guarantee I can do anything for your child. But I *can* guarantee that without my help your child will die within the next forty-eight hours."

Turn to page 40.

"Get a lab coat," she tells someone.

In minutes you feel a cotton coat being draped over your body. To your surprise, you almost fill it. You realize how fast you are growing.

You try to speak. "I'm—I'm—hun—hungry."

But before the words leave your mouth, Emily screams in horror. With a look of shock, she backs away from you.

"What's wrong?" you ask, surprised. You turn and see your reflection in the tall stainless steel cabinet beside Mr. Scully's desk.

"Oh, no!" you shriek. "This is impossible!" You blink and look again. But nothing has changed. Your reflection in the metal cabinet shows you're human again, but like no other person in the world. You have six arms, three on each side!

You bring your hands to your face. All six cover your mouth and nearly suffocate you.

Behind you, you hear Mr. Scully shuffle toward the cabinet.

"Oh, dear, I guess I slipped up," Mr. Scully says with a nervous laugh. "I wonder if I can turn you back into a fly. Would that be all right?"

The End

Almost in a trance, your mother takes the paper and signs it.

Dr. Mowbray turns to the other doctors and asks if anyone has any moldy cheese.

"What?" your mom asks incredulously.

Dr. Mowbray faces her. "The rapid expansion of mold appears to be the inverse reaction of what has happened to your child. I'm hoping to stimulate a return to normalcy by feeding the patient mold spores," he explains. "It works on similar principles to a dry sponge. Add water to the sponge, and it will expand. I plan to add spores that multiply at an incredible rate to do the same. If my hypothesis is correct, your fly will be a human in a matter of minutes. If not, we'll just have to try something else."

Everybody in the room is dumbfounded.

Dr. Joyce is the first to speak up. "I'm not sure that makes sense, Doctor."

"I'm not trying to make sense. I'm trying to save a child!" Dr. Mowbray fires back angrily. "Now hurry. We don't have much time. I don't know how long this child can live as a fly."

Turn to page 59.

You cry out again, but this time all you hear is a strange buzzing in your ears. It's a steady humming sound, almost like the noise made by a refrigerator. And once it begins, the itching and pain lessen. The sound is calming, and you relax, chalking up the experience to a bad dream. You vow never to talk about bugs with Emily again. In no time you've drifted off to sleep.

The next morning your mom bangs on your bedroom door. "Wake up!" she yells. As usual, you curl into a ball and reach for the blankets.

But there are no blankets. You reach down, and all you feel is the sheet pulled taut beneath you. Reluctantly you open your eyes. Everything looks different. You blink.

Your bedroom has grown in size. Your bed seems as long as two football fields. Your whole body covers only a minuscule swatch of the pillow.

What is going on?

You scream. But all that comes out is "BZZZZZZZZ"!

Turn to page 62.

A strong breeze from the open bus windows plasters you to a poster advertising laser surgery on warts. For the first time in your life you actually feel that wart-infested people have it lucky. At least they can go get their warts burned off with lasers. Which in your book is pretty cool. Instead, you're a fly, just about the lowest form of life on the planet. Anything is better than being a fly.

The bus slows down for a red light. Emily has her head buried in a book as you rest on the window ledge beside her. After a couple of minutes the bus jerks into motion. Whoa! You lose your balance and fall out the window!

You catch yourself just before you fall under the bus's tire and become a road pancake. But by the time you get your balance, the bus is already halfway down the block. Frantically you try to catch up, praying that the bus will stop to pick up a passenger.

The bus, however, is picking up speed. No one seems to be getting on or off. You look around and discover you're in the industrial district, a part of town you're not really familiar with.

Turn to page 50.

You do a loop-the-loop. Then you suspend yourself upside down. Luckily, you don't feel sick to your stomach at all. You can't help yourself, you're enjoying this fly stuff. As you circle your room, all you can think is, this is really cool!

Then you realize that if you're a fly you can't be in the school play. All right! The one thing you've been dreading for weeks is out of the question!

You spy some crumbs from a cookie you snuck up to your room a week ago. Breakfast! You swoop down and begin to lick a tiny, stale cookie crumb. What a feast!

Thump. Thump. Thump. The sound of footsteps on the stairs warns you someone is coming. You hope whoever it is will go to someone else's room. You need time . . . time to figure out what has happened to you. How did you turn into a fly? Can it be reversed?

The door to your room bursts open, and Emily barges in. She never knocks.

"Hey!" she yells as she skids to a stop. "Where'd you go? Your mom said you were still upstairs."

Turn to page 74.

You're a fly now. You're attracted to things that flies like, like rotting food. What can you do?

Nothing, really. So you dive in. What's so bad about half-eaten hamburgers, slippery brown lettuce, mushy tomatoes, and moldy bananas?

It's a regular feast, and you're not alone. There are literally hundreds of flies in this Dumpster, picking at delicacies such as greenish-yellow chicken pieces, soggy french fries, and dozens of other foods too spoiled to identify. And you even spy a few of your former enemies: slugs.

You eye a swarm of flies hovering over a particularly enticing paper plate of mashed potatoes, cola, and big chunks of pineapple. Worst of all, you begin to think you understand what they are saying. All the flies are buzzing in one great din, *"Food, food, food, food, food, food, food!"*

They're chanting it like a group of crazed cheerleaders when you realize you're screaming, "Food!" too. It's like one giant pep rally!

FOOD! FOOD! FOOD!

Turn to page 88.

Emily grabs a pen from Dr. Joyce's pocket, drops it on the floor, and smashes it with the heel of her shoe. She bends over and picks up the crushed pen and shakes a big gob of blue ink onto the gurney's paper sheet.

Without any prompting, you dip your front leg into the ink and write simply and clearly: *HELP!*

Dr. Joyce frowns. "How did you teach it to do that?"

Emily begins to cry. Tears stream down her cheeks. "I didn't teach him anything, I swear," she sobs over and over.

You watch in shock. The last thing you want is to be stuck as a fly for the rest of your life . . . especially a fly's life, since they live only a couple of days!

Emily catches her breath long enough between sobs to say, "Ask him anything. That'll prove I'm not lying."

To placate Emily, Dr. Joyce asks you, "Okay, what's your favorite subject in school?"

You write, *GYM!*

Dr. Joyce laughs. "I guess this fly must really be a kid. Only a kid would give that answer."

Turn to page 55.

46

A dumpster is not your ideal eating place, regardless of what form you're in. But believe it or not, you're going too fast. You can't stop in midair, and you fly right into the cold, metal side of the Dumpster.

SMACK!

You drop to the ground. It takes you a minute or two to gather your senses. You raise yourself on wobbly legs, but your head is spinning too fast to fly. You wonder if flies can get concussions. If they can, you have one.

Still a little woozy, you hop around, trying to clear your head. Your stomach growls, reminding you that you were in search of a snack when you ran into this Dumpster. You remember that you were following a smell. An incredibly delicious smell. You hold your nose up in the air to see if you can catch the scent.

Mmmmmm! You attempt to lift off, having completely forgotten your decision not to feast on rotting leftovers. Furiously flapping your wings, you rise about a foot off the ground and then veer to the right, back into the Dumpster's side. You struggle violently and swing to the left toward a brick wall.

Turn to page 23.

You take two deep breaths and gently but firmly lift your left wing. The sticky web stretches with it, not letting go. You try your right wing with the same results. You're stuck and stuck good.

"Aaaggghhhhh!" you scream, desperately looking around for the spider that made this trap. The web's silky thread sticks like cotton candy to your cheek. It feels really gross. You try to brush it off, but all six of your legs are pinned down.

Suddenly a glistening thread arcs out over you, landing across your body. "This can't be happening," you buzz-whisper. But it is!

You realize that if this spider wraps you up, you're dead. Just then the next filament comes spiraling down from high in the air above you. You deftly twist and dodge it. Almost immediately another thread comes flying down. Again you follow its slow descent and swing your body out of the way. This dance continues several more times, until out of the corner of your eye . . .

A *huge,* black, hairy spider comes crawling into view!

Turn to page 29.

48

You *have* to get her attention. You buzz around her head and land on her nose. Even though you crawl up her cheek and just avoid being smacked, Emily's eyes never leave the mask. When something catches Emily's eye, it's nearly impossible to distract her.

As a last resort, you fly under the magnifying glass, between it and the mask.

"Holy cow!" Emily immediately yells.

You hover dead center beneath the magnifying glass, desperately trying to get her attention. You know if she just looks she'll see the strangest fly she has ever laid eyes on. You're certain that she'll recognize you, even though you're a fly now. She has to notice that your head is covered with blond hair. How many flies are blonds?

From the other side of the magnifying glass, Emily looks like a monster to you. Her eyes are as big as planets. Her nose could cover the state of California. You see her massive eyelids close in a blink. Reflexively, you duck. The magnifying glass makes Emily's face seem as if it's only millimeters from you.

Turn to page 6.

50

Desperately you try to follow the bus, but your small, wildly flapping wings are no match for a bus that is cruising ten miles above the speed limit.

It isn't long before you're ready to collapse from exhaustion on a fire hydrant. As you rest, you begin to panic. Emily is your only connection to the human world.

She is the only one who knows you're not just any fly. And now you've been separated from her.

You estimate that you're ten miles from the hospital, but you doubt you can make it that far. Your wings just don't have that kind of stamina.

In the meantime, another bus zooms by, almost sucking you up in its wake. This gives you an idea. Why not wait for another bus at the stoplight and ride that one to the hospital?

Delighted by your powers of reasoning, you buzz back to the stoplight and wait. And wait. And wait. No bus comes. As usual, the buses are not running on schedule.

Turn to page 8.

You're reminded of all the times Emily stayed after school to do experiments in Mr. Scully's lab. The way Emily talks about Mr. Scully, he's a genius. Everything Emily knows about bugs she learned from him, so he must be good.

Emily grabs her knapsack and heads out of her room. "Come on, or we'll be late for school." She bounds down the stairs like some enormous dinosaur. Her mother is yelling something but you don't hear what it is because Emily nearly slams the door into you.

"Hey, Emily, remember me? Your best friend, the fly?" you buzz-shout in disgust. "Well, if you want me around, you'd better be more careful." You know Emily can't understand you, but you say it anyway.

Hearing your buzzing, Emily turns around. "Come on! We'll be late, and you know Mrs. Whittemore won't stand for me missing homeroom for the third time this week."

Emily is always late for school, which means that you're always late, too, because the two of you walk to school together.

Turn to page 57.

The bell for the first period rings and interrupts Mrs. Whittemore's announcements. Everybody dashes out of the room, relieved to be set free of her clutches.

Emily's next class is math. The halls are packed with kids opening lockers, bunched together talking, and heading for their next class. As Emily weaves through the crowds, you fly above, trying to keep her curly brown hair in sight. It's difficult to do because she's so short, and it gets even worse when Walter Smigley, the school's five-foot-ten, three-hundred-pound giant, joins the throng.

Smig steps between you and Emily, and you end up stuck in metal shop class behind Smig instead of with Emily in math. You try to scoot back into the hall, but the teacher has closed the door. You decide to wait the class out and catch up with Emily in the hall between first and second periods.

You find a nice safe corner to wait out the class. But you discover that there is no safe place in the room today. Kids are pulling on helmets and lighting welding torches.

"This is not good," you say, panicking.

Turn to page 81.

"I'm outta here!" you buzz to yourself. You fight to move down inside the hat—it must be a surgical cap—to see if you can get past the elastic rim. You wiggle and slide down to the edge and manage to squeeze under the elastic band. You tell yourself not to look down. You want to avoid looking at any patient who has his stomach cut open.

The woman whose hair you've been trapped in says, "Somebody scratch my temple."

You look up. A small metal surgical tool is coming right at you.

"No!" you buzz-scream and land on her shoulder.

"Hey, there's a fly in here!" someone says. The nurse quickly brushes you off her shoulder and tries to swat you.

"Get that fly—and fast," says an angry voice. "I don't want it landing in this stomach cavity and contaminating the patient."

Once he says that, you can't help looking. You've always been squeamish, but somehow the red sticky mess of guts looks *inviting*. Yum. It reminds you that you're hungry.

Turn to page 66.

54

Smack! goes the flyswatter again.

That was too close. So close that the breeze from the flyswatter passing by sends you spinning toward the linoleum floor. Like a small propeller plane caught in a tornado, you try to pull up. But it's futile. You bounce off the floor at dizzying speed.

To your surprise, you're not hurt. You're a little stunned. Your brain feels as if it's spent ten minutes in a blender, but nothing's actually broken.

You twitch and writhe on the floor until you get your bearings again. Then you decide to try to get your mom's attention one more time before you give up. You have to have a plan, though. Think, you tell yourself. What would convince your mom that you're not the disgusting, irritating insect she's so intent on crushing?

Before you can come up with a plan, you're fighting to save your little fly butt. A giant sneaker is falling exactly where you're lying!

Turn to page 27.

Relieved, you fly up to Emily's shoulder to try to comfort her in your small way.

"Let me consult with a colleague and see what he has to say," Dr. Joyce says, hurrying out of the examination room.

A few minutes later the door swings open and half a dozen men and women wearing white coats and stethoscopes crowd into the room. Dr. Joyce asks Emily to explain everything.

Emily dutifully tells her new audience about your uncle and the mask he sent you and what happened when you woke up this morning and all the other terrifying details.

When Emily finishes, Dr. Joyce turns to her colleagues. "The remarkable thing is that this fly still has the mind of a kid. Watch this." She turns to you and asks, "What's your favorite food?"

You quickly write, PIZZA.

The doctors press to examine you and pepper you with questions. You're beginning to feel like a circus act as you try to answer.

Fortunately, Emily interrupts. "Do you think you can turn him back?"

Turn to page 35.

56

Quickly you come to the conclusion that your mom is pretty deadly with a flyswatter. So you drop a couple of feet and fly low, out of her line of sight.

Frustrated by your mom's inability to recognize you, even if you are a fly, you decide the better strategy is to head back upstairs to your room and wait for Emily. You tell yourself that *she'll* know you . . . she never misses anything.

On the way up the stairs you notice the spiderweb that's been hanging in the corner of the stairwell for months. You vow to knock it down as soon as you're human again. Those webs can be deadly.

Grateful to be out of danger, you cruise back into your room.

You hover close to the mirror and notice that you still have your own hair. You start to laugh because you've never seen a blond fly before.

But then you remember that it's you. You're the fly. You stop laughing.

Turn to page 43.

At school the homeroom bell has already rung, and the halls are empty. Emily scurries down to Mrs. Whittemore's class with you close behind.

"Emily!" Mrs. Whittemore bellows. "You're late again." Mrs. Whittemore is the most dreaded teacher in the school. Everyone calls her "Mrs. Wit-no-more" because she has no sense of humor.

"Sorry, Mrs. Whittemore," Emily says as she slumps into her chair. "It won't happen again."

"That's right, it won't," Mrs. Whittemore says, scowling. "I'm calling your mother this evening."

Skulking along the edge of the room, afraid that Mrs. Whittemore might spot you, you make your way to Emily's desk.

"You owe me big time," Emily whispers.

"What?" you buzz.

"You won't get out of it just because you're a fly," Emily continues angrily. "As soon as you're a human, I'm going to make you pay."

"Emily!" Mrs. Whittemore shouts. "Would you please quiet down? I have some important announcements."

Turn to page 14.

"No!" Emily pleads. She points to you, and you flutter in front of Scully's face to get his attention. "See that fly? It's not! I mean, that's no fly! That's—"

Mr. Scully puts his hand over Emily's mouth just as his eyes cross and lock on you hovering before his nose. "Shhhh!" he whispers. "I see what you mean."

Mr. Scully's thick, Coke-bottle glasses must really magnify because you get the distinct feeling he can see your face clearly. He holds out his hand for you to land on. Carefully he carries you over to his desk. He picks up a magnifying glass and examines you more closely.

"Hmmm," he mutters after a minute. "Finally a student who *has* to be in my class." He laughs to himself.

You answer with an angry buzz.

"Now, now, now," Mr. Scully says, waving his finger at you. "Temper, temper. If you want to turn back into a student, you'd better be nice."

"Mr. Scully, you've got to help!" Emily begs.

Turn to page 18.

The doctors all flee the room in search of moldy cheese as Dr. Mowbray turns to Emily and your mom to explain further. "You see, I recently read a paper in *Modern Entomology* about similar genes in mold and the *Diptera transmograe*. According to this article, these genes function almost exactly alike in that they expand and change the cell structure at an incredible rate. I'm very curious to see if this theory will work."

Your mom shakes her head. "I still don't understand. You're saying some hunk of mold is going to bring my baby back."

You almost gag at the thought of swallowing a mouthful of cheese mold. And at being called *baby*.

"In short, yes," Dr. Mowbray answers. "But it's much more complicated than that. The article wasn't specific about what might happen if a *Diptera transmograe* was actually fed spores."

"So a person could die?" Emily breaks in.

The doctor nods. "It's possible, but mold is harmless in small—"

Turn to page 63.

60

To your horror, Emily leaps toward the bookshelves and grabs a paperweight. You try to move, but you're still too wet. Emily raises the paperweight high. There's a fierce, maniacal look on her face as she brings it down on your favorite pen. Then she shakes a drop of ink from the pen onto a piece of paper.

"Dip one of your legs in the ink and write what you want to tell me," she says, picking up the magnifying glass.

You grin from eyeball to eyeball. You knew Emily would know how to solve this.

On the paper in a faint, spidery script you write, *READ THE LETTER.*

Emily hunts around your desk until she finds your uncle's letter. "What went wrong?" she asks. "What did you do?"

You shake your head and shrug.

Emily doesn't understand and points to the page. "Write," she commands.

DON'T KNOW. PUT MASK ON LAST NIGHT. WOKE UP A FLY.

Whew! It was hard work writing all those words. You hope Emily doesn't have any more questions right away.

Turn to page 19.

"It's simple," Mr. Scully says as he pulls a book off his shelf. "If I can find an enzyme that breaks down this type of cell wall, our little friend here just might spring back into his old self." Mr. Scully starts flipping through a book on microbiology.

"Here it is!" he shouts after a few minutes.

The entire class stops working on the quiz and looks toward the front of the room.

"Go on, go on." Mr. Scully waves to the class. "Finish up. You only have a few minutes left."

All the students begin writing furiously.

"I have just the trick," Mr. Scully says as he pulls beakers and test tubes from a drawer. He lights a Bunsen burner.

You hope he doesn't plan a fly barbecue.

Mr. Scully begins to heat some of the sticky liquid he poured on you earlier until it boils over. Then he draws it up into a glass dropper.

"This might hurt a little," Mr. Scully says absentmindedly. He drops a small drop of the liquid on you.

"Agggghhh!" you scream as a boiling hot drop as large as Niagara Falls nearly drowns you.

Turn to page 73.

62

You move to get up and unexpectedly fly into the air! Turning to see what happened, you realize you are hovering several feet above the bed. Your body has disappeared! You don't see yourself in the mirror. All you see are your posters and shelves crammed with stuff. Then you notice a small dark speck in the mirror. You move in for a closer look. It's a fly . . .

And it's you!

This can't be happening. It's against the laws of science! Totally freaked out, you stare at yourself long and hard one more time in the mirror.

There's no doubt about it—you're a fly!

It must have something to do with the mask that Uncle Bill sent you!

Your first thought is to buzz downstairs and get your mom. She'll know what to do. But on second thought, maybe that's not a great idea. She won't recognize you. And she hates bugs more than you do!

If you want to get your mom,
turn to page 9.

If you decide to figure this out on your own,
turn to page 43.

Another doctor bursts through the door with an old cheese sandwich held in his hands like an offering.

"Perfect," Dr. Mowbray says, and places the sandwich in front of you.

Approaching the disgusting-looking sandwich, you stick out your tongue and give it a lick. You try to swallow, but it isn't easy. Mold is not your favorite food, even as a fly. You take another bite and work hard to hold it down.

"I think I'm going to be sick," you say, expecting it to come out as a buzz.

"What was that?" Emily asks.

"I said, I think I'm going to be sick!" you repeat.

Emily starts jumping up and down. "I understood him! I understood!"

You look around the room, and everyone is smiling. You look down at your legs and see only two.

You're back! You check yourself to see if you're all there. And you are!

All the doctors in the room begin slapping Dr. Mowbray on the back and congratulating him on his success.

Turn to page 76.

It smells divine. For once you're glad you're a fly. Otherwise you'd probably be sick from the aroma. Everybody knows how bad hospital food is.

Making sure the coast is clear, you dive for the mashed potatoes. Your feet sink into the squishy, warm mush.

Mmmmm. Your tongue darts down into the potatoes and laps up a tiny portion, large enough to fill your stomach.

Now it's time to sample the macaroni and cheese, your favorite. You hope it's as tasty as your mom's. She makes it right out of the box and follows the instructions perfectly. It's the only thing she makes that you like.

The sticky orange cheese coats your legs and begins to pull you in.

"It's alive!" you scream as you start to slide into the center of a piece of macaroni. The hole yawns wide open as you fight to spread your wings and lift off.

This time you're not so lucky. You're sucked deeper into the noodle. The cheese is as slippery as grease—you can't get any traction. Instead, you slide farther down into the goo.

Turn to page 30.

The breeze of a hand almost knocks you out of the air.

Get out! Get out! you tell yourself. It's hard, but you pull yourself away from the delicious-looking guts and head out the door.

In the hall, you begin to search for Emily. You can't figure out which way you came. Being caught in that woman's hair totally disoriented you.

"This hospital is too big," you mutter as you fly aimlessly around the halls.

People are hurrying up and down—orderlies pushing gurneys, nurses delivering medicine, and doctors rushing to emergencies. It makes your head spin.

You've got to find Emily, but at the same time you don't want the hospital staff to see you. Flies don't belong in a hospital—they'll make bug juice out of you!

You cruise down one hall and then another. You come to a big window and see a roomful of the cutest little babies ever. It's the nursery, where newborns are kept. It has a big picture window so that people can come and ogle them. You fly in to get a closer look.

Turn to page 7.

"I'm not sure," Emily answers disappointedly. "I've got to get to class." She pulls her math book from the locker.

NO GOOD! you write. **CAN'T HANG OUT HERE.**

Emily looks puzzled. She's not sure what you're talking about.

You dip your leg in the ink again. This is definitely getting tiresome. You wonder how Thomas Jefferson ever wrote the Declaration of Independence with a quill pen. But it has to be done. **TOO DANGEROUS AT SCHOOL,** you write.

"Oh," Emily says, as she realizes what you're worried about. "You're probably right. You'd better go home and wait there. I'll get Mr. Scully to come to your house after school— even if I have to kidnap him!"

THANKS, you write in reply.

"Do you think you can make it back home?" Emily asks with a worried look.

You picture the short three blocks. **SURE.**

Promptly at 3:15 P.M. Emily barges into your room. She throws her knapsack on your bed, not noticing that you're resting there, and almost beans you.

Turn to page 79.

Emily whips the package out from under you and tears it open. You hover above and see a letter and a small envelope. As Emily opens the letter, you read together:

Hi!
I guess it wasn't such a great idea to send you that mask. If you haven't already found out, the mask really does turn people into flies. If this has happened, the enclosed envelope holds an antidote. It's a fungus that grows on grain down here. But if you haven't already, DON'T PUT ON THE MASK!

The rest of the letter explains how to clean the mask so that it is no longer dangerous.

"It's a little late to be telling you this," Emily mutters.

"Open the envelope!" you buzz-yell.

Your buzzing gets Emily's attention. She opens the envelope and shakes some brown dust onto the surface of your desk.

Turn to page 78.

DON'T WORRY. JUST GET BY THE NURSE FIRST, you write.

"Yeah," Emily says loudly. "One step at a time!"

The people in the waiting room look at her as if she's crazy, but Emily doesn't notice. She just dashes to the nurses' station again.

Emily starts banging on the counter and yelling, "Hey! Hey! Can I get some help here? I'm sick! I think I'm going to die!"

The gorilla-shaped nurse thuds over. "What's wrong?" she asks.

"I've got this horrible pain up here," Emily says, pointing to her head. "I think my head is going to explode!" She grabs her head and moans.

The nurse pulls out a stack of forms. "Here, fill these out and a doctor will see you as soon as he can," she says. "And we need to call your parents."

Emily looks at the forms and moans really loudly. Then she swoons and falls to the ground as if she's fainted.

"Orderly! Take this girl to examination room four, pronto!" the nurse yells.

Turn to page 82.

70

In the meantime you put the mask away, do your homework, practice your lines for the play, and mess around with your favorite video game until it's time to get ready for bed. For some reason, your scalp feels itchy.

Once the lights are out and you're about to fall asleep, the itching becomes worse. It spreads from your head to your shoulders to your arms and legs. It feels as if thousands of insects are crawling on you. You think of the slugs you saw in the garden and imagine being covered with them. Slugs chewing your skin to a bloody pulp.

The itching eventually becomes so unbearable that you call out to your mom for help. Your voice sounds strange, though, and no one answers. You try to climb out of bed, but suddenly you're unable to move. Instead, your body levitates an inch or two off your sheets! And the itching keeps getting worse! All you seem to be able to do is rub your arms and legs together. It helps a little but doesn't stop the pain.

Turn to page 41.

Dr. Joyce holds up her hands. "Wait. Wait. Wait." She turns and sticks her head out of the door. "You'd better get psychiatric in here, pronto. We've got a live one," she tells someone.

"No!" Emily pleads. "I'm not crazy." She grabs a funny-looking instrument with a magnifying glass from the doctor's coat. "Look!" she demands as she holds the magnifying glass over you.

After a little hesitation, Dr. Joyce moves closer and peers through the magnifying glass.

"My word!" she exclaims. "How can that be? A fly with blond hair and human eyes." She bends down for a closer look. "This goes against the laws of nature . . ." Dr. Joyce's voice trails off as she prods you with a cold metal instrument.

You jump in surprise.

Dr. Joyce turns to Emily and says, "This is a joke, right?" She looks at you again. "How did you get that blond hair on a fly? You're pretty clever."

"It's for real," Emily pleads. "That fly is really a human. You've got to help us!"

Turn to page 45.

Your head throbs so loudly you can no longer hear anything else. You're growing larger and larger. The macaroni tube suddenly becomes too tight and bursts open!

In a panic, you start to scream. "Agghhh!" And it's not quite a buzzing sound. Your scream sounds almost like your own voice. You glance down at your body. It's no longer covered with black hairs. Your skin is changing back to human skin. Your fly legs are disappearing, and in their place arms and legs and feet and hands are sprouting!

You can feel the weight of your body dramatically increasing as you sink into the macaroni, squishing everything into a pulp.

A woman dressed in white wearing a hairnet plows through the doors from the kitchen. "Call security!" she screams, running back through the doors. "Somebody's wallowing in the macaroni and cheese!"

"Yes!" you shout in exultation. You're a human again!

And lying in a large tray of macaroni and cheese! In the middle of a hospital!

All alone!

The End

"What are you doing?" Emily gasps as you writhe in the petri dish.

"Don't worry," Mr. Scully says reassuringly. "I'm just trying to break down the cell walls. You see, the human part is still there. It's just been squeezed into the tiny body of a fly."

As Mr. Scully explains, you begin to feel strange. Your body starts to tingle and swell.

Abruptly, Mr. Scully places you under the microscope again and whistles. "It just might be working."

You nod in excitement because you're feeling a distinct change. Your body feels bloated, as if you've drunk too many sodas. Then your legs start to swell until they're about to burst. At first you think it's just your body pussing up from being boiled alive. It feels like you're getting hives.

But Mr. Scully is smiling. "Good. Good. Good."

You feel yourself gaining weight. Expanding like a dry sponge dropped in a puddle. But different. Very different.

"Yes! Yes! Yes!" hisses Mr. Scully.

Turn to page 83.

You desperately buzz around Emily to get her attention. You get it all right, but not the way you wanted. Her hands are waving crazily around her face. She immediately opens the window to shoo you out.

You avoid her waving hands and veer away from the window. You're glad Emily truly is a person who wouldn't hurt a fly.

"Enough already, Emily! It's me. I've turned into a fly!" you scream. But Emily can't understand you. All she can hear is an irritating buzz that simply gets louder when you talk.

Emily is about to leave. Then you get a great idea for attracting her attention.

You see that the window is slightly frosted from the dew. It's perfect for writing a message. Quickly you drag your body across the wet, frosted window and draw the letters *EMILY* with an exclamation point.

But Emily is looking the other way. She has found your uncle's mask and is examining it with your magnifying glass.

"Cool—a fly mask," she says.

Turn to page 48.

"But Mr. Scully . . . ," Emily implores.

Mr. Scully has already turned his back. "We've talked this over a thousand times. I just can't cover for you anymore. Now get to your class."

Mr. Scully pushes Emily out the door of the classroom and announces the experiment that the class will be doing today.

You sit on a lab table, stunned by Mr. Scully's response. Emily is his favorite student. It never occurred to you that he would give her the brush-off. You start to fly out the classroom door but realize it's shut. Mr. Scully closed it behind Emily.

As you settle into a corner to wait out the period, Emily opens the door one more time.

"Out!" yells Mr. Scully, pointing to the hall.

Emily holds the door open long enough to let you out. You give her an appreciative buzz and land on her hand.

"I *knew* you were still in there!" She carries you over to her locker and sets you down near the pool of ink on the notebook.

You hop onto the paper and write, *WHAT NOW?*

Turn to page 67.

Dr. Mowbray graciously accepts the accolades. As he opens the door to the examination room to bow out, your little brother, Jake, bursts through the door. He crashes into Dr. Mowbray's legs.

"Mom!" Jake cries and then stops midstep.

Everyone in the room is staring at him in shock. It can't be. But it is. Jake is wearing the fly mask.

Your mom screams and faints.

You flop back down on the gurney. "Here we go again," you moan. "Hey, Doc, you'd better get some more of that cheese. It looks like we're going to need it."

The End

You land next to it and begin to eat. It's pretty foul-tasting, but from the first bite you can feel a change come over you. It's as if you're a magnet and the molecules in the room are converging on your body. Your head swells, and your torso follows. Then your arms and legs begin to define themselves. Your wings fall off like dead, flaking skin.

"It's working!" Emily screams. "You're becoming a human!"

You can feel your fingernails growing and the hair on your head filling out. It's amazing how quickly it happens. In a matter of minutes you're back to your normal size, perched on top of your desk.

Emily begins to laugh hysterically.

"What's the matter? Am I all here?" you ask. You look down at yourself. *"Agggghhhh!"* Your arms and legs are covered with sharp, bristly black hairs. Thousands of them!

Emily doubles over with laughter. "On the bright side, you're a human again. Maybe the hair will fall out after a while."

"I hope so," you answer, happy to hear your voice and not a buzz. "At least it's better than trying to find pants with six legs."

The End

You fly up toward the ceiling where it's safe.

Emily circles the room looking for you. "Mr. Scully wouldn't come," she says. "He said he had an emergency and we would have to talk tomorrow."

You land on your desk and buzz as loudly as you can. You might be stuck like this forever!

Emily sees you hopping frantically on a small package. It came in the mail this afternoon. After your mom brought it up, you saw a Brazilian postmark on it. You've been waiting anxiously for Emily to arrive—maybe it's from Uncle Bill!

Turn to page 68.

Suddenly a doctor bangs through the door in an incredible hurry. Before she even sees Emily, she asks, "Okay, what's the problem?"

"Uh . . . uh . . ." Emily is at a loss for words. All she can do is read the doctor's name tag, which says DR. JOYCE. She doesn't know how to explain what's happened.

Excitedly you buzz in the doctor's face. She tries to brush you away. "Somebody get in here and get rid of this fly!" she calls out.

"Noooo!" yells Emily. "Don't kill the fly," she begs. She points to you scurrying toward the corner of the room as fast as you can. "The fly is my best friend."

You land on the examination table next to her and nod emphatically. But the doctor doesn't notice you.

"What?" Dr. Joyce asks.

Emily tries to explain in a rush of words. "The fly is my best friend. We live next door to each other and we hang out every day together. He's not really a fly. He's a human who's been turned into a fly. His uncle sent him a mask from the Amazon, and it had special powers that turned him into a fly."

Turn to page 71.

Smig holds his torch up in your direction as he focuses the flame. He flips down his mask and begins to weld two sheets of metal just below your perch. Hundreds of tiny sparks shoot into the air.

This wouldn't be so bad if you were normal size, but being a quarter inch long makes the avalanche of sparks more like a meteor shower. You find out quickly that flies don't blister, but you don't wait around to see if they barbecue.

You dart up to a bank of fluorescent lights, grateful that you weren't fried.

When the bell rings, you dash from the metal shop as fast as you can and backtrack to Emily's math class. You discover that she has already left and spot her walking to her locker between two taller kids.

"There you are!" Emily says with relief as you land on her hand. "I thought I'd lost you for good. I was so worried, I don't think I heard one word in class."

You buzz as loudly as you can in appreciation.

Turn to page 86.

A short, skinny orderly who looks as if he couldn't lift a feather wheels a gurney over and gently lifts Emily onto it. Then he pushes her into a brightly lit room filled with cabinets full of supplies—gauze, tape, surgical equipment, and strange instruments that resemble tools straight out of *Frankenstein*.

Emily lies completely still.

You hover out of the way nearby, watching the whole scene. You can't believe how good Emily is at faking it. She doesn't even let her eyelids flutter. "Wow!" you buzz in admiration.

But Emily doesn't move. Not even a twitch of her nostril.

Once the orderly leaves, you and Emily are alone in the examination room. You're thirsty. You haven't had anything to drink since a puddle on the sidewalk outside the hospital.

A faucet is dripping in the sink in the corner. You land by the drain and suck up some water.

SPLASH!

A huge drop nearly washes you down the drain. In a panic you hop to the lip of the sink.

Turn to page 24.

You glance over at Emily. She's jumping up and down excitedly.

Mr. Scully lifts the slide you're on and places it gently on the floor behind his desk. He's giving you room to grow out of sight of the class.

Suddenly you're cold. Your skin begins to change back to its normal color. You can sense your hands coming back and your legs extending. It's all happening very slowly.

You look up and see that Mr. Scully is no longer next to you. He's talking to his class. Everything seems far away. You don't know where Emily is. Your body is changing too fast for you to process the environment around it. At the same time, it feels as if your transformation is taking an excruciatingly long time.

In fact you've lost track of time. You don't know if the class has ended and another has begun. All your energy is focused on your body's growing flesh.

Your head pounds as blood pulses through your veins. You can feel your stomach expanding at an alarming rate.

After a while you notice Emily hovering over you.

Turn to page 38.

84

Even though you're flying as fast as you can, you're having a tough time keeping up with Emily. This flying isn't as easy as you thought. You collapse on her bed and try to catch your breath.

For a minute you think Emily has forgotten you. Then, as she stuffs her math book into her knapsack, she explains her plan. "Don't worry," she says, trying to comfort you. "I bet Mr. Scully will have some ideas. He has a master's in science, and he loves bugs."

Turn to page 51.

You make a headlong leap for the tomatoes and land on the fleshy part of a juicy slice.

Ahhhhhhh. The answer to your prayers. The excruciating pain quickly lessens to a dull, barely noticeable throb. You wallow in the cool comfort of the mushy tomato slice . . . take a couple of delicious nibbles . . .

Squish!

You've just been pulverized against the counter along with the slice of tomato. The heel of your mom's palm grinds you into the hard surface. Now you're just a stain on the countertop. For eternity.

Your mom wipes your remains away, throws out the tomato, and finishes making lunch. And you're history.

The End

Emily sits on the floor in front of her locker and pulls a pen out of her pocket. She bites the end hard, breaking the pen open. Ink spills down the corner of her mouth as she shakes some onto her notebook.

"We've got to talk," Emily whispers. You land next to the puddle of ink, ready to write. "I've got English, art, and lunch before science," she says.

You begin to worry. That's too long to wait! You start writing furiously on Emily's notebook, *CAN'T WAIT THAT LONG.*

Emily nods. "That's what I think, too. We've got to talk to Mr. Scully now. Before the next class starts."

The two-minute warning bell for the next class period rings.

"Come on!" you buzz and start down the hall toward the science lab.

"I'm right behind you," Emily says as she shoves her books into her locker, being careful not to spill the ink, just in case you need it later.

Turn to page 16.

As you join in the frenzy, your thoughts of returning home and finding Emily begin to recede. Memories of your uncle's mask, your room, and your favorite baseball mitt all become hazy and distant. You can no longer imagine what your mom and dad look like, let alone your bratty brother. You don't remember that you're supposed to be in the school play this afternoon. So you can't even have the pleasure of knowing you're going to miss it.

Before you can understand what is happening to you, you're raving just like the hundreds of other flies feeding in this Dumpster. Obsessed with only one thing: *Food*. Luscious, succulent, pungent, rotten morsels.

Your life before this moment is forgotten. You're a fly. That's all.

BZZZ.

The End